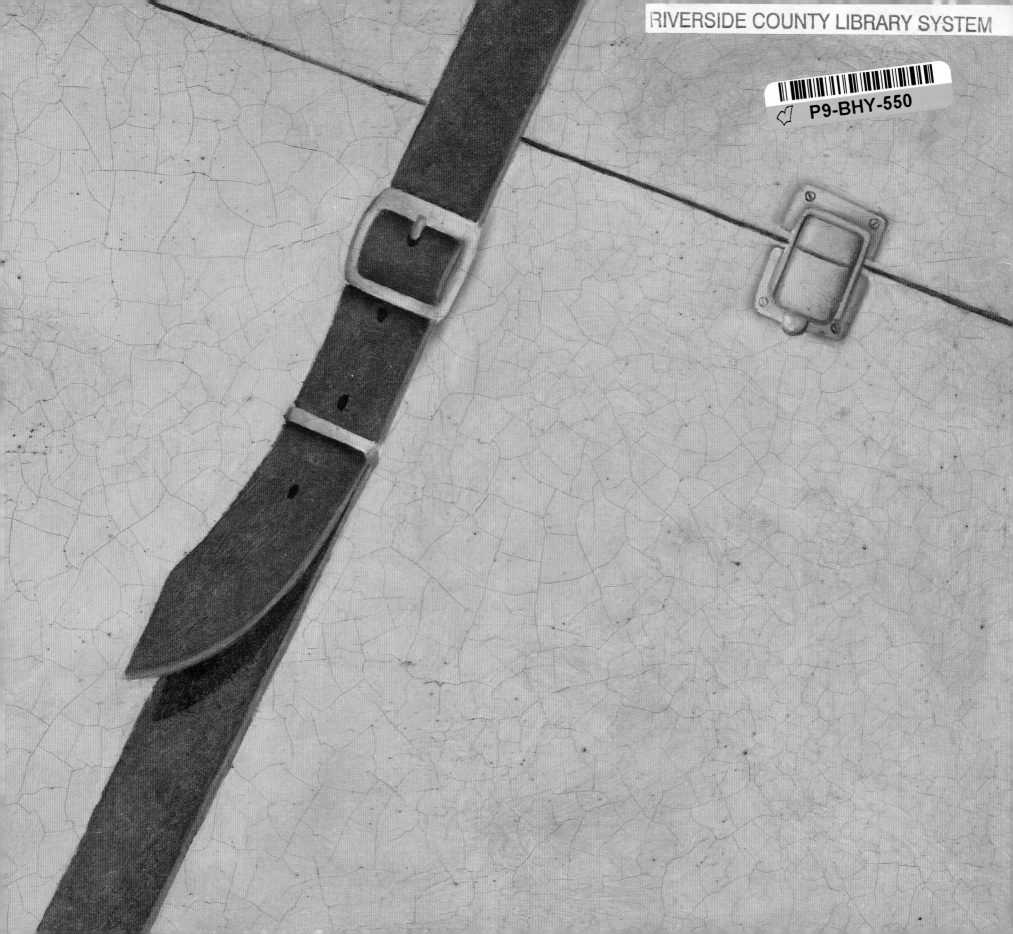

First published in the United States in 2002 by Chronicle Books LLC.

Text and design © 2001 by the Templar Company.
Illustrations © 2001 by Alison Jay.
Originally published in the U.K. in 2001 by Templar Publishing,
an imprint of the Templar Company plc, Pippbrook Mill, London Road,
Dorking, Surrey Rh4 1JE, U.K.

North American text design by Jessica Dacher.
Typeset in Filosofia, Eidetic Neo and Zemke Hand.
The illustrations in this book were rendered in
alkyd paint with crackle-glaze varnish.
Manufactured in Belgium.

Library of Congress Cataloging-in-Publication Data
Repchuk, Caroline.
The race / Caroline Repchuk ; illustrator, Alison Jay.
p. cm.
Summary: A modern rhyme retells the events of the famous race
between the boastful hare and the persevering tortoise.
ISBN 0-8118-3500-6
[1. Fables. 2. Folklore.]   I. Aesop. II. Hare and the tortoise.
English. III. Jay, Alison, ill. IV. Title.
PZ8.2.R355 Rac 2002
398.24'52792–dc21
2001003883

Distributed in Canada by Raincoast Books
9050 Shaughnessy Street, Vancouver, British Columbia V6P 6E5

10 9 8 7 6 5 4 3 2 1

Chronicle Books LLC
85 Second Street, San Francisco, California 94105

www.chroniclekids.com

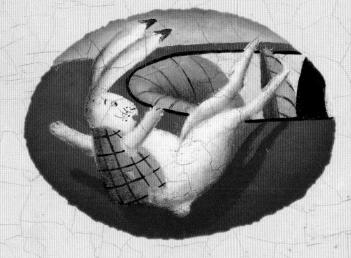

The Race

by Caroline Repchuk · illustrated by Alison Jay

chronicle books · san francisco

Tortoise and Hare each packed a case.
To New York City they decided to race.

Honk!

tooted Hare, "I want to go fast."
But steady Tortoise crept on past.

"Hey there," Tortoise answered. "Want some advice
that you should consider once or twice?

Slow and steady is the way
to get somewhere without delay."

"No," said Hare, "I like a fast pace!"
And so began a famous chase.

A bet was made. A route was set.
"Let's go," said Hare. "I'll beat you yet!"

Hare revved up at the starting line,
while Tortoise simply took his time.

"See you in New York I trust?"
said Hare, leaving Tortoise in a cloud of dust.

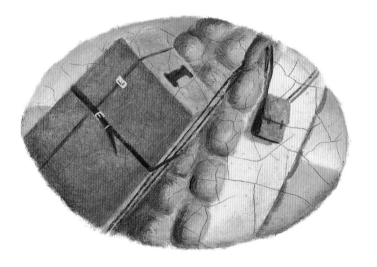

But Tortoise had a cunning plan,

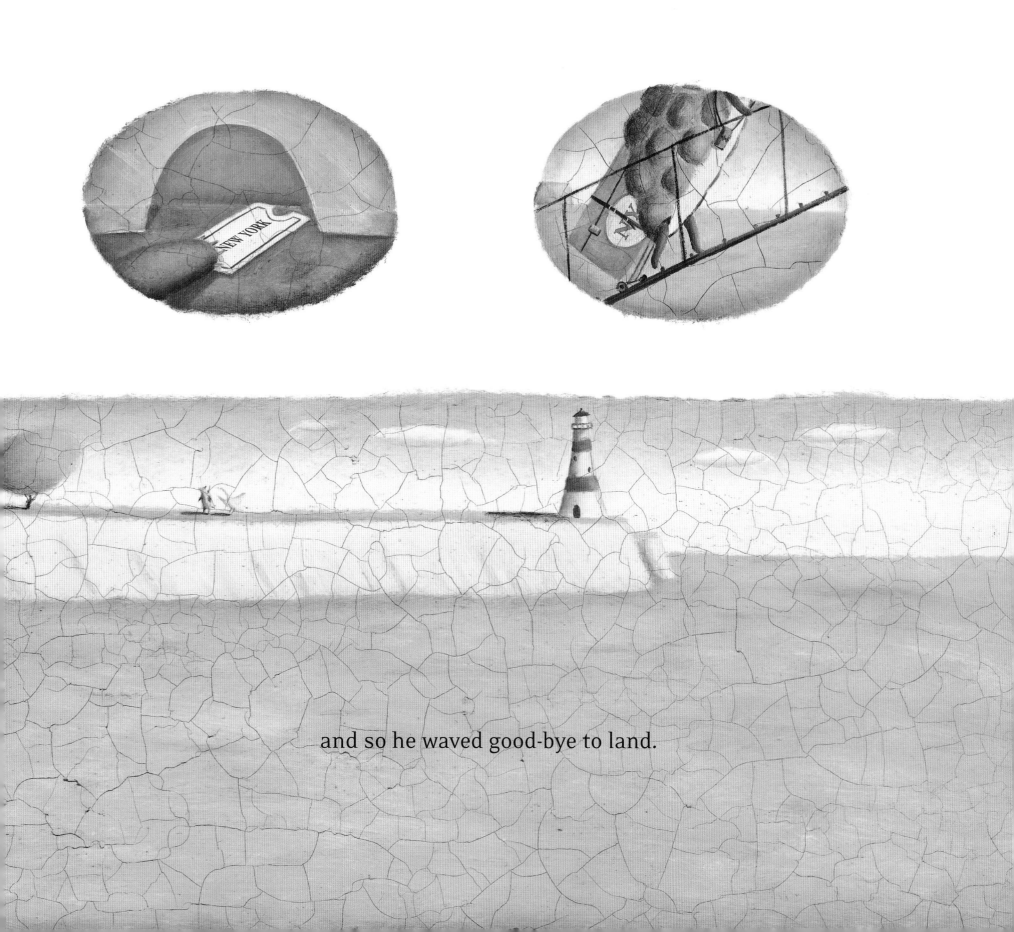

and so he waved good-bye to land.

Although Hare had set off on the double,
he very soon ran into trouble.

Swiftly Hare flew out of town,
but **what goes up must come down.**

And as he crawled across the land,
    a suitcase clutched in his tired hand,
    the only thing that he could think

was, "Gosh! I really need a drink
                    of…"

"…water!"

Hare shot down the raging river. That poor old bunny was all aquiver.

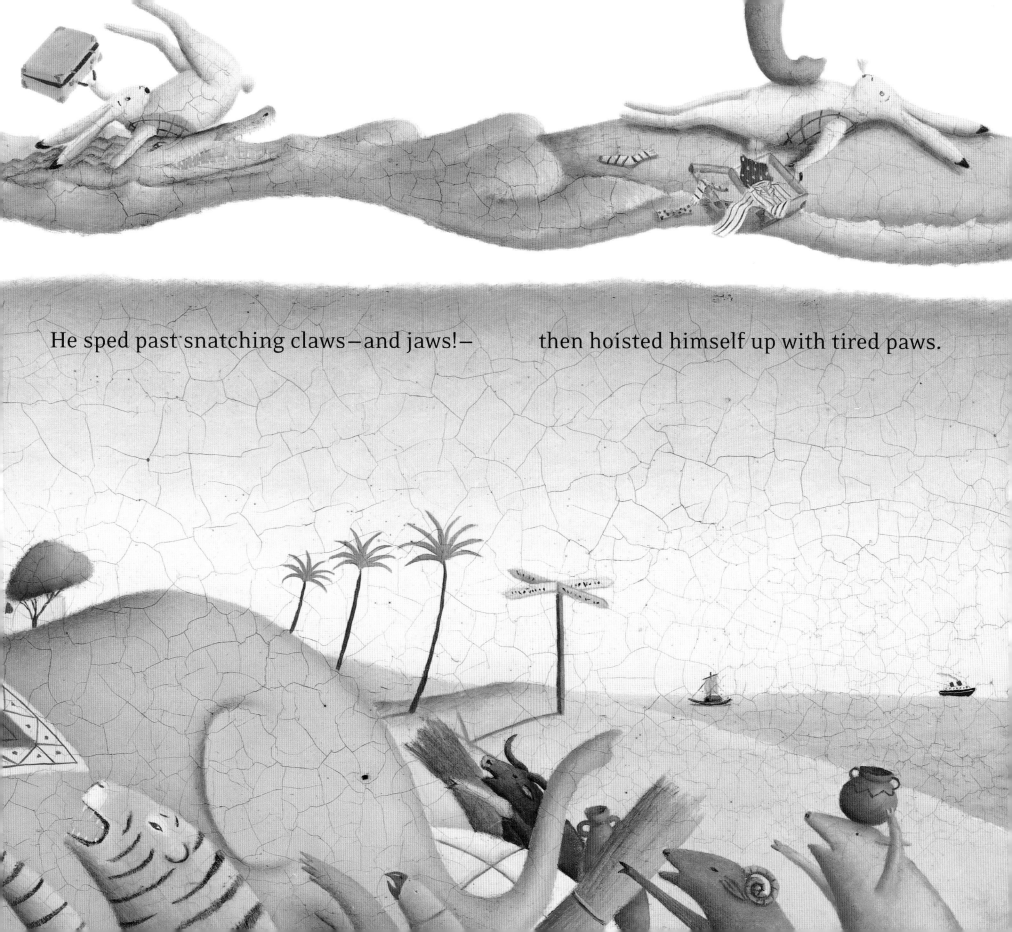

He sped past snatching claws—and jaws!—   then hoisted himself up with tired paws.

Hare's next move wasn't any easier.
He found himself all the queasier,
bound for China on a boat,
while Tortoise simply stayed afloat.

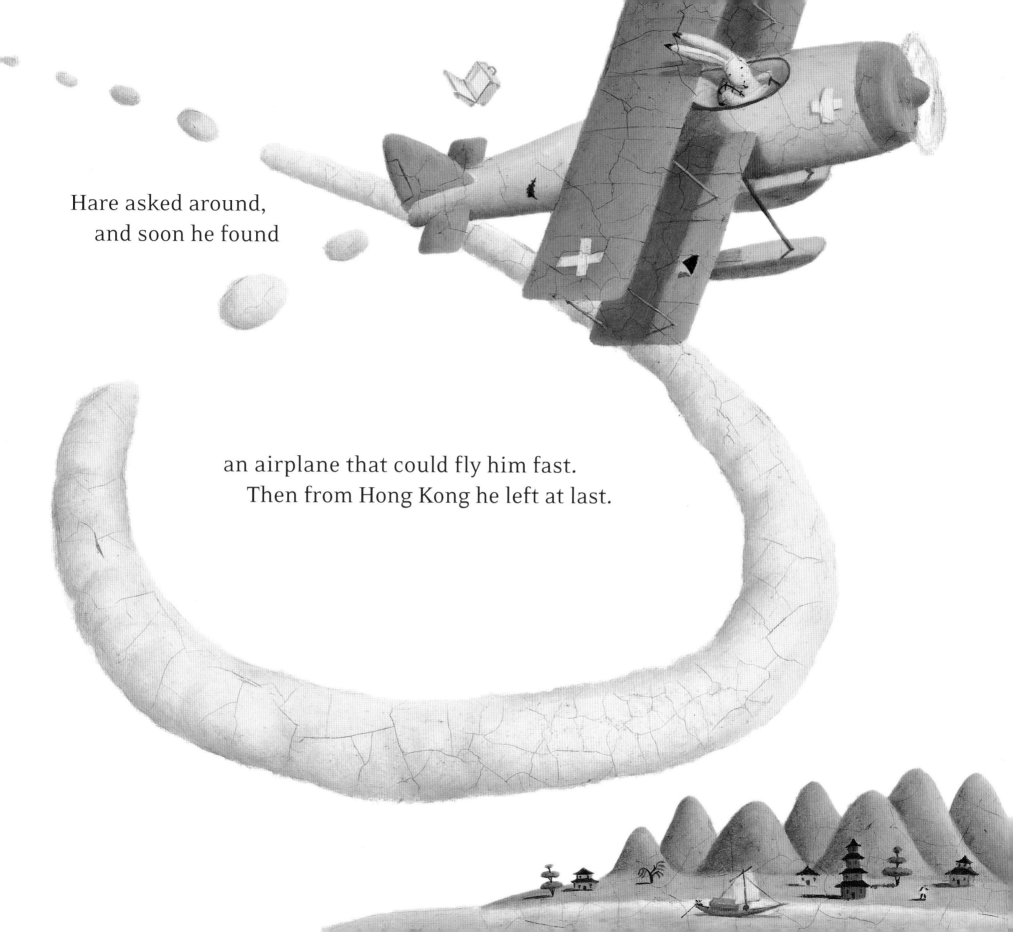

Hare asked around,
and soon he found

an airplane that could fly him fast.
Then from Hong Kong he left at last.

For days he went across the ocean,
flying with a lurching motion.

So it wasn't any wonder
that he ended up Down Under.

Now kangaroos are jumpy things
(I think their feet are made of springs),

so when poor Hare gave them a scare
by falling on them from thin air,

they thumped and bumped him
up and down
and quickly bounced him
out of town.

By surf and ski
Hare made his way

across the water   until one day,

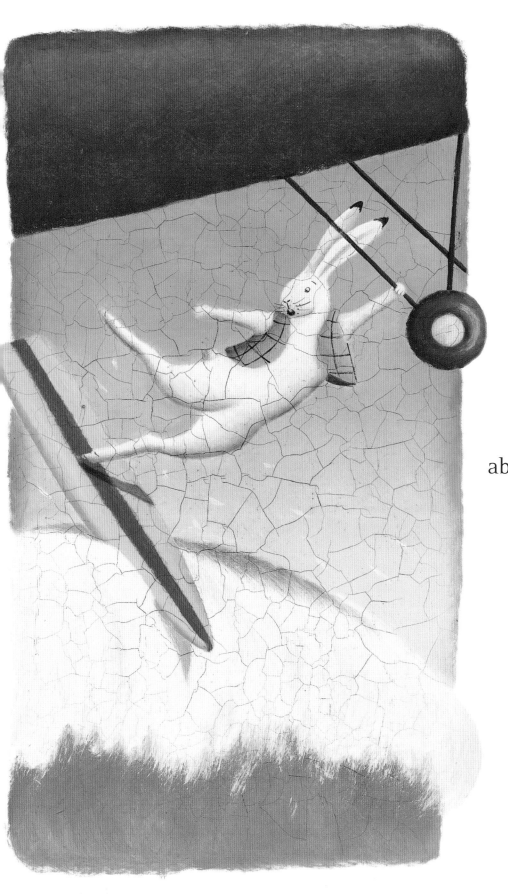

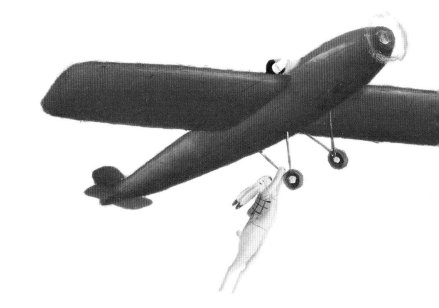

aboard another passing plane,
on Tortoise he began to gain.

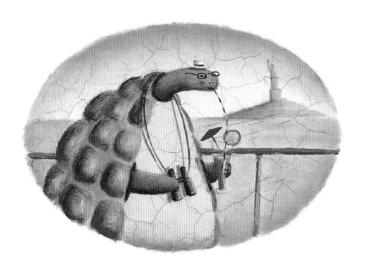

Hare was setting record time.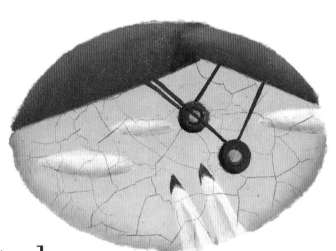
He cried, "This race is surely mine!"

But no, his goal was soon frustrated,
for in New York, Tortoise already waited.

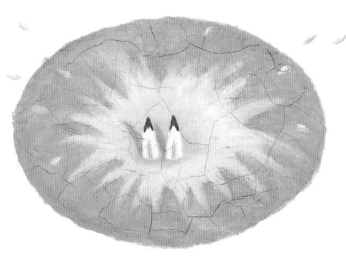

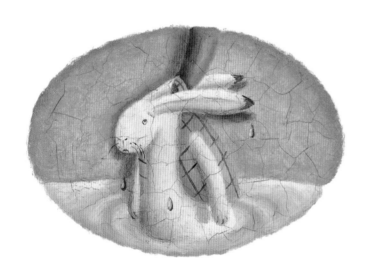

So it seemed Hare had been beat,
 and at long last admitted defeat.

Poor Hare, he was sadly deflated.
 It turned out that speed was overrated.

So the moral of the story will stay.

Slow and steady wins the day!